FRIENDS

OF ACPL

P9-BTY-183

The SONG of the LOP-EARED MULE

Books by *NATALIE SAVAGE CARLSON*

The Song of the Lop-Eared Mule
Pictures by Janina Domanska

The Tomahawk Family
Pictures by Stephen Cook

The Happy Orpheline
Pictures by Garth Williams

A Brother for the Orphelines
Pictures by Garth Williams

The Family Under the Bridge
Pictures by Garth Williams

Sashes Red and Blue
Pictures by Rita Fava

Wings Against the Wind
Pictures by Mircea Vasiliu

The Talking Cat
And Other Stories of French Canada
Pictures by Roger Duvoisin

The SONG of the LOP-EARED MULE

by NATALIE SAVAGE CARLSON

Pictures by JANINA DOMANSKA

HARPER & BROTHERS   *Publishers*   NEW YORK

For my grandson,
WILLIAM PAUL SULLIVAN

1146805

The SONG of the

LOP-EARED MULE

I

It happened in southern Spain. Most of it happened to a brown mule named Fedro.

It began in the little village of San Antonio back in the hills. Fedro belonged to a farmer nicknamed El Bigote because he was a man of spirit and mustache.

Fedro's mother had been beautiful because she was a horse. The little *mulito* had thought that he was a horse, too, until his ears grew so big. Then the first time he lifted his tail, threw back his big ears and opened his gray muzzle to whinny, he was astonished to hear a low, mournful bray.

It was "deep song," as the Spanish gypsies call their sad, piercing songs. It was a song about hard roads, heavy collars and iron shoes.

Life was hard for all the beasts of San Antonio but especially for the mules and donkeys. There was a big

I

public fountain in the square where the beasts were watered in the morning and evening. Carved on it were the words:

"Be kind to your animals. They lighten your burdens."

In forgotten years the ceremony of the blessing of the animals had taken place by the fountain on the feast day of St. Anthony. But that had been neglected, too, because the farmers felt it broke into the work day and gave the animals idle notions.

The words on the fountain became overgrown with moss and unreadable. Nobody paid any attention to them any more. The farmers forgot them, and so did the women who did their washing at the fountain.

The people of San Antonio worked hard themselves. They thought their beasts should work twice as hard because they had four legs instead of two. Only the children of the village remembered to be kind to the animals and reward them with pats and treats of sugar or greens.

The older Fedro grew, the more he looked like his donkey father. His mane never grew beyond a brush. His ears grew longer and one of them flopped over. His lower lip sagged. His tail hung like the frayed bell rope in the village church.

And he was noisier than a herd of donkeys. He brayed sorrowfully every time he thought of what a disappointment it was to grow up to be a mule instead of a horse.

His mother was disappointed with him too. Her reproachful whinny meant, "You take after your father's side of the family, not mine."

But Fedro's master was proud of him. "He has grown into a fine strong mule," he said. "Already he can carry twice his own weight on his back. And what a voice! I wish I knew what he is singing about."

"He is complaining about something," guessed his wife, Concha. "He has the same tone of voice as my great-uncle Esteban when he used to complain about his rheumatism and the poor crops and taxes."

El Bigote and his wife and ten children and his wife's sister's family and all her children lived in a faded yellowish bluish pink house at the edge of the village. All the other houses were the same style and undecided color. All of them had the same tile roofs faded from bright red to a deep brown by the jealous sun, which wanted no brightness but its own.

The barn for the animals sprawled around the foot of the hill. It was circled by a rickety fence made of all kinds of things. There was even an old bed frame patching one side.

El Bigote and his families were poor but they did not know it.

"What is the difference between money and beasts?" asked El Bigote.

3

"None," he answered himself. "We have four goats traded us for Fedro's mother, a team of oxen, a strong young mule and all the sky along with half of the sun and half of the moon. We are rich."

"If you don't start irrigating the fields," said his wife, "we will starve in the midst of all our wealth."

The next morning El Bigote put the plaited straw bridle and harness on Fedro and led him down the path. They skirted the garden strips and cornfields and went up an ox trail to a dirt road that wound through the low hills.

The well was near the road. It was mounted with a great iron wheel on which hung rusty tin buckets. Two long handles stuck out from the wheel, one higher than the other and ahead of it.

El Bigote hitched Fedro in front of the low handle and fastened a rope from the higher one to his bridle. Then he tied an old sack over the mule's eyes.

"Now you are going to Granada," said the farmer, giving him a light blow with his stick. "He who sees Granada sees paradise. Giddap, Fedro! It is a long way to Granada."

So Fedro lifted his pointed hoofs and started the long trip to Granada. But the handle on his bridle kept him going around and around. And the handle hitched to his harness started the water wheel going around and around. As the wheel turned, it lifted buckets of water. When they hit the rim of the well, they spilled into the ditch and started a stream flowing down through the hills to the garden below.

Then the farmer went down to work in his fields and left his mule all alone on the treadway of the water wheel. But Fedro didn't know he was going around and around. He thought he was pulling a farm wagon on the long road to Granada. He pulled with all his might and walked at a lively pace because he was so proud to be going to Granada.

Once a shepherd and his sheep passed on a nearby trail. The bells on the sheep jingled merrily and the shepherd's dog barked at Fedro. Now and then a farm wagon pulled by oxen or mules would go down the road toward the village. Fedro's big ears turned toward the rumble of the wagon wheels and the clopping of the oxen or mules. He thought that he was passing them on the road to Granada.

That evening his master returned, unhitched him from the wheel and took the blindfold off his eyes. Fedro was surprised to find himself at the well again. He turned his long ears and stared down the road that led away through the

6

brown hills. He thought it had been a long, hard trip to Granada. He was proud that he had made it all by himself, even if he hadn't seen anything.

Every day El Bigote took him up the trail to the well. Every morning he hitched him to the water wheel, tied the blindfold over his eyes and told the mule that he was going to Granada.

And all day long Fedro thought he was on the long road that went around the world. He was a hard-working mule and he did his best. Even a proud bull fighting in the arena can't do more than that.

But one day El Bigote was in such a hurry that he did not tie the blindfold securely. Fedro started out on the long road to Granada. He passed the sheep and the rumbling farm carts with their clopping beasts. Then the sack began to slide down from his ears.

It slid under one eye and the sight that eye saw made Fedro dizzy. The hills and mountains were going around and around. It fell from the other eye and Fedro clearly saw that he wasn't going to Granada at all. He wasn't going anywhere. The handle over the well was leading him around and around in a circle.

Fedro was filled with rage at the shabby trick his master had played on him. His father's temper flared. He tore his head loose from the bridle. He lowered it between his forelegs and set his hoofs flying through the air. He kicked and kicked until the handle behind him was splintered and the tin pails churning a whirlpool.

He lifted his tail and his head high into the air. His deep song echoed through the hills. It sang of man's treachery and unfairness to mules.

He kicked up his heels and went running away to join the antelopes in the mountains.

II

ALL AFTERNOON FEDRO WAS FREE. He ate the growing corn and wheat to his heart's content. At last he grew thirsty. So he searched through the ravines until he could smell water. It came from a stream that flowed through a poplar grove. Fedro made for the grove as fast as his iron shoes would take him.

Then he saw the gypsy camp. A ramshackle old van covered with faded green shingles was propped beside the stream. A skinny horse was munching what little grass it could find. A woman sat on the ground weaving a basket from reeds. Around her played a brood of ragged children of all ages.

They looked surprised to see Fedro.

"Tito," called the woman to someone behind the van. "Come quickly, Tito."

A man with long black hair and a red sash came from

behind the van. He put his hands on his hips and stared at Fedro.

"Come here, good mule," he said to Fedro. "Let me look at you closer."

Fedro walked to him with wide, trusting eyes. The gypsy man ran a knowing hand over Fedro's brown back and sides. He opened Fedro's mouth and looked at his teeth.

"He is a young mule," said the gypsy, "and sound of body. Only that left ear is weak."

The children gathered around the mule and looked at him with glittering eyes.

"Providence has sent him to us," said the woman, "because our old horse is sick."

Tito grinned. "Then I must get to work on him before Providence comes looking for him," he said.

He pulled his shears from his red sash and went to work on Fedro. He clipped all his hair so that he was a lighter brown and looked like a sheared sheep.

"That *loco* ear still looks the same," said his wife with a critical eye.

"It can be cured," said Tito. He turned to the children. "Go pick some flowers for me," he ordered.

The children scurried every which way like squirrels. They returned with purple thistles and red poppies.

"Make them into a bouquet, Lola," the man told his wife. "The proper size to put under that ear to brace it."

Lola's nimble fingers made a red and purple bouquet. Together the pair tried it this way and that until it braced the ear just right. Then they fastened the bouquet into place with wire. It gave Fedro a gay fiesta look such as the beasts had once worn for the feast day of St. Anthony.

The gypsies finished none too soon. Providence came into the grove in the shape of El Bigote looking for his runaway mule. He carried a big stick and his face was dark as a winter cloud.

When he saw the gypsy camp, his suspicions were aroused. When he saw the sheared mule with a bouquet tied to its ear, he was sure that he had found his lost property.

"Thieves!" he cried to the gypsies. "What have you done to my mule?"

The children scrambled into bushes and behind rocks. The gypsy couple looked at him with astonished eyes.

"Heaven forgive you your mistake, *señor*," said Tito politely. "This is our own mule, isn't it, Lola?" he asked his wife.

The woman nodded. "Why would we want somebody else's mule when we have our own?" she asked sullenly.

El Bigote's mustache quivered with anger. "It is my Fedro who ran away from the water wheel," he shouted. "I will have you put in jail."

Tito's black eyes rounded. "It cannot possibly be your Fedro," he said, "because this mule of ours is different from all others. He is a trick mule and with him we make our living."

"What trick does he do?" demanded El Bigote.

"He is a singing mule," answered Tito.

"My Fedro is a singing mule, too," retorted the farmer. "His bray is different from all others."

Tito smiled. "But does he sing in pure Castilian Spanish?" he asked. "My mule can sing an entire ballad about the Cid with every word as clear as glass."

El Bigote uneasily looked at the clipped mule with the bouquet decorating its ear. To be sure it did look different from Fedro, but there was something familiar about that long face and the ear leaning over the flowers.

"Let me hear him sing the ballad about our great hero who fought the Moors," he demanded.

Tito sadly cast his eyes to the ground. "Alas, *señor*," he said, "today my mule will not sing. He had a quarrel with my wife this morning and now he is sulking."

"A likely story," scoffed the farmer. "Now I know you are lying. This is my mule and I'm taking him home with me."

The gypsy thoughtfully ran his hand over Fedro's clipped back. He turned to his wife. "Lola," he said, "you must apologize to the mule so he will sing for the gentleman. It is the only way we can prove that he is our mule."

"No, indeed," said the woman, stamping her foot. "He is a lazy, long-eared fool just as I told him this morning."

"Hush," warned the gypsy. "He will never sing again if you keep calling him names. Please apologize to him."

The woman haughtily drew her rags together and walked away.

"You see," said the gypsy to the farmer, "I really have two mules. But if you will give me time, I will get around my wife. I promise you that I will make her apologize. If you will come back tomorrow, the quarrel will be ironed out and the mule will sing the ballad for you."

El Bigote grudgingly agreed.

As he turned to leave, Fedro lifted his tail and opened his mouth—but not to sing the ballad. He wanted to bray his grief at being fooled at the water wheel. He wanted to beg to go home to his own stable. But the gypsy man was quicker than Fedro's tongue. He sprang to the mule's hind-quarters and pulled his tail as hard as he could. Fedro was stricken dumb because any gypsy trader knows that a mule cannot bray unless he lifts his tail.

El Bigote trudged back to his house alone, stamping the earth with his stick.

He told his family and his wife's sister's family about the remarkable mule owned by the gypsies. He was sure now that it was not Fedro. That lop-eared rogue would turn up in somebody's corn before long.

The children were the most excited. They begged and begged El Bigote to take them to the gypsy camp next morning so they could see the mule that wore a bouquet on its ear and hear it sing the ballad about the Cid.

El Bigote and his families were up early the next morning. The children carried handfuls of corn to offer the performing mule. They walked through the hills to the grove at the stream. But they did not get to hear a mule sing a ballad in Castilian Spanish.

The gypsies were gone and the remarkable mule with them. Only the lame horse still munched weeds at the edge of the stream and she could only whinny.

Then El Bigote flew into a lion's rage. "The vagabonds!" he roared to Concha. "It *was* Fedro. I will go to the police. I will alert the Civil Guards. And I will give that stubborn Fedro a good beating when I get him back. Why wouldn't he sing the ballad for me? He had had no quarrel with *you*."

Concha tried to soothe him. "I will pray to St. Anthony to find our mule and bring him back to us," she said. "I will make some kind of vow."

But El Bigote would not be soothed. "Say your prayer," he growled, "but I will go to the police. And I vow that when I get my hands on that lop-eared mule, I will give him a good beating."

III

FEDRO WAS FAR AWAY from the beating. He was really tramping the road that led to Granada. The van shed more shingles at every bump in the road.

The bridle Fedro wore had blinkers. But he could see the sights ahead of him. Every noon he could see the long line of hooded two-wheeled carts carrying farm workers back to their village for the midday meal. Some of the wagons had three or four mules pulling them. Others had donkeys, and one was followed by a long-eared colt who was enjoying a short childhood. Under every wagon ran a dog leashed to the bottom.

One day they met a flock of sheep and Fedro had to stop and wait for them to go by. The shepherd shouted commands and his little dog carried them out until an old ram turned and chased it into a field.

Fedro was nearly frightened loose from his ears by a great black beast of burden that silently sneaked behind the van, then whinnied with the throats of three hundred horses. Fedro shied off the road and the black monster roared by with the speed of three hundred horses in team. The mule had never seen an automobile before.

They went over the brow of a hill. At the bottom stood a pair of Civil Guards lounging over their guns. In their

black cocked hats and green uniforms they looked like two tin soldiers cast from the same mold. But the guard standing on the right side of the road had a large nose and the one on the left had unusually large ears.

The guard with the big ears stared at the gypsy van drawn by the mule. He stared harder at Fedro's flopping ear, fingering one of his own as he did so. Then he straightened, lifted his gun and stepped into the middle of the road.

"Halt!" he commanded.

Fedro stopped because it sounded as if the man had said "whoa!"

"Now the melon has been cut," whispered Tito to his wife.

Both guards walked all around the van, carefully noting each loose shingle and each gaping hole. Then they returned to the front.

"Where did you get that mule?" asked the big-nosed guard. "The description of such a beast has been sent out. It was stolen from a farmer in San Antonio."

Tito doffed his floppy hat humbly. "There is some mistake, *señor*," he answered. "This mule has always been with us. He is one of my family."

The guard snorted. "Then you can come with us to the next village and have the police look at your long-eared relative."

18

The other guard fingered his own ear again and frowned at his companion. "We will leave the mule's ears out of this," he said curtly.

"No offense, *amigo*," said the first. "A man can't help the ears he is born with, but on a mule, ears are no mistake."

"Please, *señores*," put in Tito, "I swear by everything Christian that this is my mule. There is no other like him because he is a singing mule."

"A pretty story," sneered the guard with the big nose. "Let us hear him sing a tune."

Tito obligingly reached ahead and pumped Fedro's tail vigorously. The mule raised his head and sang his sad, deep song.

The guard seized Fedro by the bridle. "Rascal," he cried to Tito, "he brays like any other mule."

The gypsy explained. "Perhaps you cannot understand him, *señor*, because he sings in the Catalan dialect. He began a ballad about two brave Civil Guards who captured a dangerous smuggler."

The guard was impressed. "He did sound like my cousin from Barcelona when he complains about the weather and the fleas and his wife's cooking," he admitted.

The guard with the big ears turned upon him mockingly. "Only a stupid Catalan would bray like a mule," he snorted.

19

The other gripped his gun tighter. "You are speaking of my father's oldest brother's son," he retorted hotly.

The big-eared guard shoved him with the butt of his gun. "I am speaking of all Catalans," he shouted. "They are bad heads, every one of them. Nothing good comes from the province of Catalonia—neither man nor garlic."

The big-nosed guard gave him a blow on the shoulder with his gun. Both men began clubbing each other.

Tito raised the reins and clucked to Fedro. The gypsy van slowly lumbered down the road, dropping a few more shingles. They were entering the next village before they heard a volley of shots.

"They are warning us to stop," cried Lola.

"Ha! They have probably shot each other," said Tito. But he urged the mule on faster. "Giddap, Fedro!" he shouted. "Step lively, Chaco! On your way, Pepe! Faster, Luna!"

The woman looked at the single mule pulling the van. Even the children looked over their shoulders to see such a long team.

"Have you lost your mind?" asked Lola. "We have only one beast pulling the van. We left Luna in the poplar grove in exchange for the mule."

"Not so loud," warned Tito. "If Fedro thinks there are three mules behind him helping to pull, it will lighten his burden so he can go faster." He shouted at the top of his whip. "Get up, Fedro! Faster, Chaco! To the collar, Pepe! Giddap, Luna!"

So Fedro thought he was the lead mule of a four-mule team, such as he had seen along the road. He walked faster because his load seemed lighter with all the other mules helping him.

They passed the village threshing floor where teams of two mules were pulling wooden sleds weighted by great stones around and around over the grain to break it up. Fedro sang deep song and the mules answered him in a chorus.

That night the gypsies camped in an olive orchard. Tito drove Fedro to a gnarled gray tree. He took off the bridle with its blinkers. Fedro looked around to greet the other mules who had shared his work. There was nothing behind him but the gypsy van.

The mule had been fooled again. He lifted his voice in deep, sad song and every mule in the countryside answered him.

Fedro was not the only one complaining. The gypsy children were whining about the approaching Granada. They did not think it was going to be paradise.

"Why do we have to go to school?" asked the oldest boy. "I want to work in Granada and get rich."

His father shook him by the shoulder. "You will go to the school of the Ave Maria like all the other gypsy children. Do you want to be a stupid, wandering gypsy all your life?"

"Yes," cried all the children together.

Lola turned to them. "Don't you remember what that singer we met in Madrid told us? Every gypsy in Granada is rich."

"I don't want to be rich if I have to go to school," sulked the boy.

"Do you want to wander the roads all your life like a mule?" demanded his father.

"What will we do with Fedro there?" asked a little girl. "May we ride him to school?"

"Why not?" asked her father. "You shall go to school, Mother shall cook over a fine charcoal stove in a nice snug cave and I shall lie in the sun all day long."

At last they reached the richest valley in all Spain. They drove through fertile vineyards and orchards of olive and orange trees. Above them towered the snowy peaks of the Sierra Nevada mountains. And ahead of them was a city of red roofs and white houses clinging to the hillsides.

It wasn't the end of a day's walk around the water wheel. It was really Granada. Fedro had never seen such a big village, but it didn't look like paradise to him. Its streets were narrow and endless. They crossed and crisscrossed in a most confusing way. And through them honked herds of the powerful black monsters.

They went through narrow cobbled streets with iron grilles over the windows and balconies decorated with pots of geraniums and carnations. Twittering swallows swooped over Fedro's head.

Tito knew the way, and it was the steepest one in Granada. It went up, up, up between walls that hid white houses and shady gardens. It went up, up, up to the Sacro Monte with its gypsy caves and clumps of pear cactus.

The van creaked and groaned. The chimney fell off and rolled down the hill. The streets of the Sacro Monte were full of gypsy children and dogs. The children shouted to Tito's brood and the dogs barked at Fedro.

Tito stopped before a neatly numbered cave front. It had a narrow red roof over its white front and its windows were planted with geraniums. Fedro could look inside the open door and see the rough whitewashed walls and the bright copper pots hung on them.

Tito came back and jumped into the van. "There is nothing for us but a cave higher up deserted by a family that took to the road," he explained. "It is little better than a dog hole."

"All the less rent and housework," said Lola.

The children began to shout gleefully. "We're going to live like the foxes in their holes," cried the oldest boy.

"We're going to live like the wildcats in their rocks," cried a younger one.

"And I'm going to sing and dance all day long," cried the oldest girl.

"Until school starts," warned Tito.

Then they all quieted down and Fedro was brought to a stop before a bare cave with a roofing of brush. It was more like a rude stable than a cave dwelling. But it looked as good as the tumbledown van by now. Fedro saw that the actual stable was an open hole where chickens scrabbled in the dust.

The mule looked at the snow-topped Sierra Nevada mountains. He looked across the valley to the rust-colored walls of the Alhambra Palace which guarded the city like a Moorish ghost. He looked down at the red roofs and white houses, the brown walls and crooked streets. Then he burst into deep song. He did not think that Granada on its hills was going to be a mule's paradise.

IV

It did not take the family much longer than foxes or wildcats to get settled in their cave. All the gypsy children of the Sacro Monte and their dogs came to watch them unpack their rags and pots.

Then Tito gave the van a stout kick and it fell apart.

"So ends our life on the road," he stated.

His children looked sad because the van was their last chance of escape from the schools of the Ave Maria. But the other children cheered them up.

"We dance and sing in the schools," said a girl with long, uneven bangs.

"We learn to make things to sell," said a boy with blue eyes.

"Don't you have to study lessons?" asked Tito's oldest son.

The gypsy children looked less cheerful. "Yes," answered the girl, "but I have a pretty teacher. She's a gypsy, too, so she knows we'll get sick if we study too hard."

"What do you have to study?" persisted Tito's son.

"Oh, arithmetic and reading and writing," put in a girl with long braids.

"Last year we learned why the year 1492 is so important," said the girl with uneven bangs.

"Why is it?" asked Tito's son, because he couldn't see why anything that had happened that long ago could still be important.

"Because in 1492 the Catholic Kings chased the Moors out of Spain," chimed all the little gypsies in a chorus.

"Right here in Granada the Moors surrendered to King Ferdinand and Queen Isabella," said the blue-eyed boy. "I'm glad it wasn't the gypsies they chased out."

Fedro turned his long ears toward the rusty walls of the Alhambra Palace which the Moors had been compelled to leave behind.

Tito was squatting near a prickly pear bush, picking his teeth with a prickle and talking to some of the men.

"If you can dance or sing or play anything," said one of his companions, "you will get rich fast from the tourists."

Tito shook his head. "I can trim dogs and horses," he said.

"You can send your children and the mule to the Avellano spring to get water to sell in town," suggested a gypsy in a pink vest and blue beret. "Everybody wants the spring water because it is sweet and clear. My boy goes every day so he can show your children the way. It is easier to let the children make the money."

"Pah!" exclaimed another. "You can get rich faster by working steady in the new factory, making tourist souvenirs."

Tito lazily pushed his feet out in front of him, flattened his back against the ground and pulled the brim of his old hat over his eyes. "Tomorrow I will decide how to get rich," he stated.

The next morning some of the men stopped by the cave to get him to go to the factory.

"Tomorrow I will go," promised Tito. "Today I must make a gate for Fedro's stable from the pieces of the van. I will send the children and the mule with Antonio's boy to get water from the spring."

He strapped a jug on each side of the mule. When Antonio's boy came on his donkey, Tito lifted his five older children, one after another, on Fedro's back. He gave the mule a slap on his rump. "Off with you," he ordered the children, "and don't take all the water from the spring. Leave some for tomorrow."

His children forgot all about the water and the Avellano

spring because there was so much to see. They went down, down the steep road to the Cuesta del Chapiz with the little donkey in the lead. They entered the Carrera del Darro, which was like a walled shelf along the ravine of the Darro River. Of course the Darro was only a trickling stream, but one can't be too fussy about the size of rivers in southern Spain.

They met many little donkeys with tinkling bells and tasseled bridles. Some were pulling small hooded carts and others were humpbacked under loads of wood or barrels of provisions. Once they met a herd of milk goats. The owner had driven one up on a woman's steps and was milking it into her pitcher.

Across the ravine rose the red wall of the Alhambra hung with green vines. It looked old, mysterious and adventuresome—as if some of the Moors might still be hiding behind it.

"Let's go to the Alhambra," suggested Tito's oldest boy. "We can start our water business tomorrow. The spring will still be there."

So they parted company with Antonio's boy at the Plaza Nueva. They drove Fedro up the Cuesta de Gomerez until they found themselves at the entrance to the Alhambra woods.

Great cypress trees and elms towered over them. The coolness was like a breeze from the snow-capped Sierra

Nevada mountains. Birds sang overhead and fountains whispered in the distance. It was the paradise that El Bigote had promised Fedro back at the water wheel.

The gypsy children stared at the gracefully arched gates and delicately carved windows. They stared at the visiting Moorish chieftain in red cape and flowing white headdress as he walked down the path, bearing himself as straight and proudly as if his people still owned the palace. They licked their lips at sight of the stands where black-clad women sold crisp potato chips in paper twists.

Then Fedro began eating some sweet-smelling jasmine, so a stern policeman in white helmet and blue trousers drove them out of paradise.

It was hot back in the narrow streets and going home was the hardest part of the trip for Fedro. All the roads and paths that had gone down so fast went up so slowly. The rough cobbles clinked against his hoofs. The swallows twittered in his ears.

"I wish we had gone to the spring," whined Tito's littlest boy. "I'm thirsty."

Fedro slipped on the cobbles going up the Carrera del Darro. The littlest boy fell off his back.

"You will have to walk the rest of the way—like Fedro," said the others after several unsuccessful tries to get him up again.

They noticed that the donkeys climbing past them had

baggy slippers tied over their front hoofs to keep them from slipping as Fedro had done.

"Tomorrow we must make some bag shoes for Fedro," said Tito's oldest girl.

The mule slowly struggled up the hills while the boy who couldn't get back on him followed. Fedro wanted to bray his complaints about the steep hills and no bags on his hoofs to every passing beast. But he couldn't because he wasn't able to raise his tail. The little boy who had to walk was clinging to it to help himself up the steep paths.

Tito was surprised to learn that they had not gone to the Avellano spring for water.

"Tomorrow we will go," said the children, "when you go to the factory."

Fedro could raise his tail now because the little boy had let go of it. He raised his head, too, and opened his mouth. He brayed a piercing song about the hot and slippery streets of Granada.

The factory workers came to get Tito next morning.

"Tomorrow I will go with you," he repeated. "I haven't made Fedro's gate yet."

Only Lola did anything that day. "I am going to town to tell fortunes in the street," she announced. "The quickest way to get riches is to promise them to other people. Watch Fedro so he does not get into any trouble," she reminded the children.

31

For half an hour they obeyed her. They threw pebbles at the mule and pulled his ears and tail. Then they lost interest and scrambled down a trail to find some playmates.

Fedro was free. He was hungry too. He wandered over the barren hillside and ate prickly pears until his gray muzzle was stained red. Then he found out it was more enjoyable to eat geranium leaves off the window sills of the better caves. He ate some fig leaves hanging over a wall and some blessed palm festooned on a window grille. He nibbled some straw that belonged to a donkey.

So tomorrow's work didn't overwork anyone, even Fedro. He should have been satisfied, but he wasn't. Idleness breeds discontent in mules as well as men. He wistfully remembered how proudly he had carried burdens for El Bigote and how useful he had been to the country families. He remembered how hard El Bigote and his wife and his wife's sister's family and all the children had worked. He began braying more and more.

At night the gypsy caves were noisy with singing and dancing. All of Tito's family went to the gatherings. Fedro was left alone on the hillside in the stable that had no gate yet.

The mule looked across the gorge at the dark walls of the Alhambra, so black and silent in comparison to the gypsy caves. He listened to the songs of the nightingales in the Alhambra woods. He wanted to sing with the nightingales so he stood all alone in front of the empty cave and brayed so loudly that the nightingales were frightened into silence.

Some gypsies came to their doors and threw empty cans and bottles up the hill at him. They liked noise and made a lot of it. They didn't want any other noise drowning out their own.

One night they were making more noise than usual because a big tourist bus had brought a crowd of North Americans to visit the Sacro Monte. The gypsies were entertaining them in one of the big, clean caves below.

The girls had gathered from all over the Sacro Monte in their best flounced skirts and bright shawls with artificial flowers and high combs in their well-oiled hair. The gypsy men were stylish in tight trousers and bright sashes.

In command of the affair was the women's captain. She looked like a brown lizard with her dark wrinkled face and cold eyes. But she had plastered her forehead with love curls and fastened fancy combs and paper flowers into her hair so that people would look at her curls and ornaments instead of her face and think that she was beautiful.

Fedro had come down from the hillside and was standing lonesomely outside the cave, looking in the lighted doorway.

Four men were playing on musical instruments, one of which looked like a mule's collar. The gypsy girls were sitting in a half-circle, clapping their hands. The *tintirin-tín* was enough to break even a mule's big eardrums.

The captain took her turn at entertaining. Even though she was so old, her thoughts were young and one of them was that she could dance and sing. She suddenly stopped dancing because her feet wouldn't go any more. So she burst into "deep song." Her voice was high and shrill, but what it lacked in sugar it made up in pepper.

Fedro wanted to sing a duet with the captain because her voice sounded like his mother's. He pushed his shoulders through the open door. He pulled his head back, lifted his tail and joined in the captain's "deep song."

The concert came to an abrupt end. The tourists burst into laughter and the gypsies turned furiously to the door. The captain was angrier than any of them. Her feet came to life and she stamped them in rage. She pulled a guitar from one of the musicians and brought it down on Fedro's head.

The musician howled and grabbed his broken guitar from her. The other gypsies began screaming and clawing each other in the feud which Fedro had started. The Americans knocked the chairs over in their haste to escape from the cave.

By the time things had quieted down, Fedro was high up on the hill with his ears turned toward the nightingales singing in the woods of the Alhambra. He didn't join them because his head ached too much for his ears to listen to his own music.

The mule didn't know it but he had made a dangerous enemy. The old captain would have no rival. She vowed that she would cut off Fedro's tail and slit his tongue and pull his ears out by the roots. Fortunately she vowed to do all those things "tomorrow."

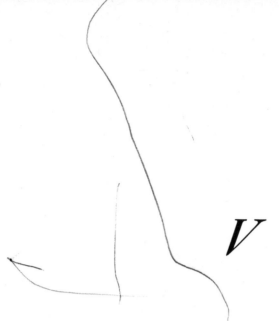

V

THE GYPSIES WHO WORKED in the factory did not give up easily. They came to Tito's cave another morning.

"Tomorrow is here now," said their spokesman. "It just arrived over the Sierra Nevadas with the sun."

"Remember the old saying," said another. " 'Nothing begun, nothing ended.' "

Tito lazily yawned and scratched his side. Somebody's old rooster up the hill had brought tomorrow, too, and kept him from getting back to sleep.

"Then I will go with you so I can make enough money to buy tickets for the bullfight Thursday," he answered. "But I will only work one day, and that will begin it and end it."

Everyone was excited about the coming bullfight because the captain's grandson, Bombita, would be one of the *toreros*. Already his pictures were pasted up in town showing him in his bright "suit of lights" with a sword in one hand and a red cape over his shoulder. And towering over him was a black bull with blazing nostrils and long sharp horns.

The children could think of nothing but the bullfight too.

"Will you take us with you?" Tito's children begged him.

"No," answered their father. "There is only money enough to buy tickets for your mother and myself on the sunny side."

Most of the gypsy children had to be satisfied with their own bullfights. The captain's great-grandson, Pablo, had made a bull for himself. It was only a wooden board but Uncle Bombita, the great bullfighter, had given him a handsome pair of long horns to fasten on one end. Next to a real bull, it was the next best thing.

Pablo would snort and stamp and push his horns at anyone who wanted to play the bullfighter. The other boys took turns facing Pablo's bull with a red rag and a wooden sword. Such brave *toreros* had never been seen in a real ring. They let the bull brush against them. They seized him by the horns. They shouted insults at him. They killed him a hundred times and died a hundred brave deaths themselves.

Fedro followed Tito's children to see the mock bullfight. He stood among the mangy dogs who sat in a semicircle like the poor fans who can afford only seats on the sunny side.

A lively fight was going on. Pablo roared hoarsely and panted as he worked his board as much like a real bull as he could. The boy with blue eyes waved his mother's red tablecloth back and forth as he dared death in the afternoon.

The other children clustered around, eagerly awaiting their turns.

"Juan, you aren't holding the sword right."

"Faster, Pablo! Your bull is slow as a cow."

"Ah ha, *toro. Olé, torero!*"

Even the dogs were taking sides. When Pablo almost horned Juan, his dog growled at Juan's dog. When Juan pointed his sword at the place on the board where the bull's neck should have been, his dog grew bold and snapped at Pablo's dog. At last the two dogs got into such a fight that Pablo had to lay down his board and Juan drop the sword and cloth to pull them apart.

When the dogfight had ended and the boys went back to the bullfight, Juan found Fedro sniffing curiously at the tablecloth on the ground. The boy picked up his sword and cloth and began dancing around Fedro. He had found a better bull than one without a body.

"*Toro,* ah ha!" he shouted. "Look at the fierce new bull. *Toro,* ahaaa!"

He waved the cloth in Fedro's face. Fedro was willing to play. He had often played chase games with El Bigote's children in the old days when he was a little *mulito* and hadn't grown big enough to work.

He began chasing the boy with the waving red cloth. The other children jumped up and down with excitement and cried encouragement to Fedro.

"Aha, *toro!* Get him, *toro!*"

Pablo with his horns on a board felt left out of it. He sulked for a little while. Then he pushed his make-believe bull between Juan and Fedro.

"Fedro isn't a bull," he decided. "He's a bullfighter. A long-eared, dumb *torero*. *Hola!*"

He shook the horns at Fedro. He began snorting and stamping again.

Fedro was bewildered by the change in the game. He wanted to be the bull still. He made a couple charges at the horns. Pablo was delighted. He gave the mule a sharp punch with them. He gave him a sharper punch.

Fedro laid back his ears and let out a shrill whicker. He whirled around quickly and lowered his head.

Pablo was frightened. He threw the board at Fedro and ran for his great-grandmother's door. The mule's hind hoofs caught the board in midair. They splintered it and sent the horns flying in two directions.

All the children went screaming up the hill. The dogs put their tails between their legs and bounded down the hill. It was as if a real bull had leaped the barriers of the arena and stampeded the spectators.

The captain came out of her cave with her love curls loose and the combs and flowers falling from her hair. She pulled off her red shawl and shook it at Fedro.

"Go away, demon!" she shouted. "On your way."

Fedro looked at the red shawl she was waving. This was the kind of bullfighting he understood and liked. He see-sawed his ears and lowered his head. He charged at the shawl.

The captain screeched and ran for her cave. She slammed the door shut just in time to escape death in the bullring.

Fedro was disappointed. He looked up the hill to where the children were crouching among the cactus pears and chimney pipes. He looked down the hill to where the dogs were barking at him from doorways and bushes. He was so bitterly disappointed that he burst into "deep song."

The captain was in a rage. She vowed that she would get rid of Fedro.

She took herself, combs and love curls and flowers, to the mayor of the gypsies. He was holding his office in the shady square because it was so hot inside. All the gypsies of the hill had followed the captain. The children had tagged along too.

The mayor was an old, old man, but he was straight as garlic and had the hearing of a knife grinder.

The captain spat and shook her fists and called the saints from above and the devils from below to be her witnesses. She gave Fedro a long string of names which did not flatter a mule. She accused him of more crimes than one mule could commit. Then she ran out of words and ended breathlessly, "The mule does nothing all day long but wander through the streets eating our plants and frightening our children. He isn't worth his ears full of water."

Then all the children came to Fedro's defense. He hadn't frightened them very much. He was really harmless.

"We need him to carry water from the Avellano spring," added Tito's own children.

"I need him to work for me," said Tito himself. "How can a laboring man get along without a beast?"

"Puf!" put in the captain. "You and your children and your mule will go to work when oxen fly."

Her great-grandson was against her too. "I was teasing the mule," he confessed. "I pushed horns at him and he didn't like it. Even a bullfighter wouldn't want to be punched by horns with no bull on them. We need Fedro to play with us."

The mayor tapped his cane and buried himself in heavy thought. It was such a hot day, and all this business about the mule had broken up his afternoon nap on the bench.

At last he finished his thinking. "The mule must be tied up," he said. "It must not be allowed to roam loose."

Tito's lips lifted into a big smile. He bowed and bowed to the mayor.

"Tomorrow I will build a gate in front of his cave," he promised. "No rope is strong enough to hold Fedro when he wants to roam. That is how I came into possession of him."

The mayor pointed his cane at Tito. "*Today* you will build the gate," he ordered. "Not tomorrow."

Tito's smile turned upside down. He sighed and left with his children. The captain flounced away without saying *oxte* or *moxte*.

After Tito had rested enough for the job, he built the gate from scraps of the van which Lola hadn't used for firewood yet.

"Alas!" he said when he had finished. "Now we will have to feed him. He won't be able to get into anyone else's hay or graze on the hill."

"We will let him eat weeds along the way when we go to the spring of the Avellano tomorrow," said his oldest son.

"That is a good idea," agreed his father. "Tomorrow you can take him there while your mother and I are at the bullfight."

The children were uphappily reminded that there was not enough money to get them into the arena. They hung their heads. They wished they had gone to the spring faithfully. They could have saved enough money from selling the water. They might even have saved enough to buy tickets on the shady side. Now it was too late. One tomorrow had come too soon and the other too late.

VI

ON THE GREAT DAY of the bullfight, Tito's children sadly watched the other gypsies getting ready to go into town. The captain wore more combs and flowers and love curls than usual since her grandson was to be the main bull-fighter. Of course her great-grandson, Pablo, was going with her to see his Uncle Bombita win his fight with the bull.

"We can't go," Tito's oldest boy told him. "We didn't earn any money for tickets."

Pablo looked at him sympathetically. "It will be a great tragedy if you do not get to see my uncle fight the bull," he admitted. "Why don't you go down into town and beg for money?"

"Beg for money?" asked Tito's boy, surprised that he hadn't thought of it himself.

"Sure," said Pablo. "People are generous on a bullfight afternoon because they are happy and they want everybody to be happy. Look sad when you beg. Pull yourself together skinny. Look hungry and poor." He critically looked at Tito's children with their rags and dirty faces. "You should get a lot of money," he encouraged them. "You're the poorest-looking children I've ever seen."

The gypsies streamed out of their caves, the women in their long gaudy skirts and the men in their big hats and tight trousers.

Tito and Lola had cleaned themselves for the great event. Lola had even sewed some new patches on their old clothing. But the children made no effort to better their looks. Gleefully they led Fedro out of the stable. It was a long way to the Square of the Bulls so they were lucky to have a beast. They climbed on his back from an overhanging rock, one after another. The younger ones who had to stay behind howled with grief.

Off the older ones set for the town below, the kind rich people and the bullring. Fedro went down the winding roads with his ears akimbo. He skirted the Albaicín and clinked into the busy streets where the crowds were larger and noisier. They went through some streets so narrow that the children could nearly touch each side with their bare toes.

At the Plaza de San Nicolás, they gasped at the beautiful view of the Alhambra and the Sierra Nevada. It was like the postcards that peddlers sold to the tourists. But they didn't stop to look long.

Down the long wide Cuesta de Alhacaba they went. They took a short cut through a side street to the old Moorish gate of Elvira. Suddenly the noise of the crowd grew louder, like thunder over the Sierra Nevada. There were shrill screams of terror.

"A bull!" someone shouted. "A bull has escaped from the arena!"

"Run for your lives!"

"Help! He is coming this way!"

"Indoors, everybody! Out of his way!"

The street in front of Fedro emptied like a broken water jar. He could see the great black bull. It was racing to meet them, snorting and tossing its horns.

Tito's children saw the bull too. It looked like the one on the poster with Bombita. They jumped and fell off the mule's back. They raced through a door that a man held open for them.

Fedro faced the bull alone. There were no *picadores* or *banderilleros* or barriers to protect him. But there were plenty of spectators to see what was going to happen to him. They were peering out of grated windows and leaning over balconies. The bull came closer and closer to Fedro. Bulls have poor eyesight so he probably thought that the mule was a horse and that he carried a *picador* with a long lance. He stopped and pawed the cobbles warningly. He shook his long sharp horns at Fedro.

Those horns had a familiar look to the mule. He remembered the day he had played bullfight with the gypsy children. He remembered the pair of horns that had punched him.

The bull came charging at him, just like Pablo's board. Fedro laid back his ears and showed the bull his teeth. Then he wheeled around and raised his hind legs. He showed the bull his iron shoes.

Whack! Crack! One hoof caught the bull in the middle of the forehead and the other snapped off the tip of his left horn.

The bull sat down on his rump. He was dizzy and bewildered. He didn't know if he had been hit by a lance, a sword or a bolt of lightning.

He bellowed and raised himself from the cobbles. He charged again. Fedro gave him the kicks of ten mules. They caught the bull on the nose, the chest and the forehead.

The bull stood in the middle of the street and bawled for sympathy. He had never been treated like that by a horse before. Then he turned tail and ran back to the bullring because he thought he would be safer there.

Fedro was as unhappy as the bull. He raised his tail and he raised his head. He sang his deepest song. They had

made him play the bullfighter again when he wanted to be the bull.

Then wild cheering filled his long ears.

It was as if Fedro were a popular *torero* in the bullring. The people threw things down to him to show their admiration. They threw flowers and combs and fans. What made the children happiest was that they also threw coins. Quickly the little gypsies came out of hiding and scooped up the money.

Fedro should have become the most popular mule in Granada.

Unfortunately the captain's grandson was pitted against that very bull when it returned to the arena. All the fans burst into laughter at the ridiculous sight of the broken-horned bull with the swollen nose and shut eye.

Bombita didn't like the looks of the bull either. It didn't look funny to him. It moved about in a *loco* way and had a queer, dazed stare in its open eye. After a few rounds of playing it with the cape, the captain's grandson decided that the bull had the evil eye. It would bring him bad luck. No one wants to tempt bad luck less than a bullfighter.

Bombita remembered the old Spanish saying that it is better to say "Here he ran" than "Here he died." The gypsy kept as far away from the bull as possible.

Whistles shrilled from the spectators because they had not spent their money to watch a man dancing away from a bull all afternoon. They began throwing things at Bombita. Not fans and combs and flowers but hard things like bottles and rocks.

So fast does news travel in a Spanish town that already many had heard of the bull's meeting with Fedro.

"Bring on the mule!" shouted some of the fans.

"The fighter is afraid of the bull," cried others. "Bring the brave mule. *Olé, mulo!*"

They whistled at Bombita scornfully. Neither he nor the bull won the fight.

Little wonder that the bullfighter burst into his grandmother's cave that evening with his temper striking sparks.

"Bring on that mule!" he shouted. "I will give him my last sword thrust."

It took all the coaxing of the captain and her pretty dancing girls to keep him from making Fedro play the bull again.

"We must do this legally, Bombita," his grandmother reminded him. "If you take the law of the Sacro Monte into your own hands and kill the mule of another, you will become an outcast."

Bombita stormed and raged some more. Then the pretty girls reminded him of his past triumphs in the bullring. They told him that he was handsome and graceful and daring. They told him that he was better than a mule.

But the captain and Bombita went to see the gypsy mayor

the very next morning. This time there was no hope for Fedro. The people who had cheered him in the streets did not come to his rescue. Not even the children dared say a good word for him. He had spoiled a bullfight. In Spain there is no greater crime.

"You must get rid of him," the mayor ordered Tito.

Only Tito's children whined and sobbed.

"What will happen to Fedro?" they asked fearfully.

"Must we push him over a cliff?" asked Lola.

"No, no," answered Tito. "That would do no good to us or Fedro. He will have to go back to pulling the collar again. I shall sell him at the cattle market."

So poor Fedro had to pay the duck, as the Spaniards say of one who is punished unjustly.

VII

TITO WANTED FEDRO TO APPEAR at his best for the cattle market. He fussed over him as if he were a gypsy bride. He trimmed the mule's hoofs and brushed his tail until it snapped with electricity. He tinted Fedro's coat a richer brown.

When Fedro looked as handsome as a mule could look outside, Tito began fixing him inside. He chopped garlic and red peppers together and made them into pellets. He forced the pellets down the mule's throat.

They burned Fedro's mouth and throat at first. When they were down, they made him feel as frisky as a colt. He wanted to gallop and kick and fight some more bulls.

The children tearfully told Fedro good-by, then hurried back to their games with no more thought of him.

Tito leaped on Fedro, sitting back on his croup as if he were riding a donkey. He grabbed for the rope around

Fedro's neck and away they went. Fedro bolted down the hill and through the lazy streets, looking for a bull to fight. His hoofs clicked like castanets against the cobbles. The surprised donkeys stopped in their tracks at sight of such a mule. The people on foot pressed against the walls to give him enough room. Fedro raced a big bus and leaped over a wine barrel that had rolled into the middle of the street.

He rushed out of the city to the banks of the Genil River where the gypsies held their cattle market. He might have run all the way to the Mediterranean Sea if the river hadn't stopped him.

The market was alive with beasts but there was not a single bull. There were donkeys with ears longer than Fedro's. There were sad-faced mules and short-eared horses. There were even a few oxen and a flock of dirty sheep.

Yesterday these beasts' masters had taken the stick to them and called them names. Today their masters could not speak well enough of them.

"You see the fine coat on this horse, *señor*. She is gentle as a lamb and strong as an ox."

"My little donkey is all patience and loyalty. And would you believe it? He hardly eats a handful of hay a day. He would rather work than eat."

"This mule's teeth may be old but he has the muscles of a yearling."

Fedro quieted down a little. He turned his eyes and ears toward all the sights. He saw the crowds of farmers and idlers surrounding each beast. He saw a man having a fight with his horse, and the horse was winning it. He saw the dark-skinned gypsies in their gay rags and tags and the farmers in their sober work clothes.

Soon everyone saw Fedro too. The snack Tito had given him wouldn't let him stand still for long. He switched his tail and kicked his hoofs and tossed his ears. He felt as if he were full of live eels.

"That's a right lively mule you have there," said a farmer. "Is he broken in yet?"

Tito looked at him shrewdly. "Is he broken in?" he asked back. "I can tell you that it took me a year to do it, he was so strong and spirited. Now he can't be still. He wants to pull a plow or a wagon all the time."

A crowd gathered around Tito and his spirited mule. Everyone wanted to look into Fedro's mouth and feel his muscles. But when Tito told them the price of such a good mule, no one wanted to buy him.

"He is probably unruly," said one.

"He has a crooked ear," said another.

"He has a mean look in his eye," said a third.

Tito sneered at them. "Whoever expects to find a perfect mule should go on foot," he quoted an old proverb.

Then a strange-looking man elbowed his way into the circle. He wore a long black cape and his thin hair grew to his shoulders. There was a pointed beard at the bottom of his face and a slouched hat on top of it.

He ran his fingers down Fedro's long face. "A worthy Dapple to team with my Rosinante," he declared. He turned to Tito. "Knoweth thou Don Quixote?" he asked.

"No," answered the gypsy, who had never read the book about Don Quixote's adventures because he couldn't read at all. "I have seen his statue in Madrid and his windmills on the plains of La Mancha, but I have never met him."

He was puzzled by the man's manners and words. He tried to figure out his business. He couldn't decide whether the stranger was a gentleman or a smuggler. As the Spanish say, a cape covers many things.

"What price do you set on these mismated ears?" asked the man, pointing to Fedro.

Tito gave him a keener look and decided that the cape was so shabby that it must cover a smuggler.

"My mule may have a crooked ear," he said, "but his hoofs carry him silently as a cat's paws. He is sure-footed and he knows when to keep his tail down. Two thousand *pesetas* and he is yours with no questions asked."

The man in the cape pushed Fedro's crooked ear. "I will give you a thousand *pesetas* for him," he said. He pulled out the bills. The gypsy held his hand out as if to receive them, but let them fall on the ground. *"Amigo,"* he said, "I am selling the whole mule, not one of his ears. Fifteen hundred *pesetas* and he is yours."

The man stooped and picked the bills out of the dust with a flourish. "I am a poor actor, not the governor of Granada," he returned. "Don Alonso of the Traveling Theater. I will give you twelve hundred *pesetas*."

Tito saw that he had made a mistake. He turned his tongue on the other side. "My mule may be a silent fellow most of the time," he said, "but he has a golden voice. He really belongs on the stage instead of in harness."

"My company of players is already full of asses," said Don Alonso. "What I need is a strong beast to pull one of my wagons. Twelve hundred *pesetas* is all that I can pay. And that is robbing my actors of their week's wages."

"With a mule that sings as beautifully as this one," said Tito, "you would not need any other actors in your company. He will make you rich."

Don Alonso was curious. "Let me hear him sing a tune."

Tito obligingly pumped Fedro's tail. The mule parted his teeth and sang a deep, deep song. He sang it with a breath full of garlic and red peppers.

Don Alonso scoffed. "He is braying like any other mule," he said.

"It is little wonder that your ears are plugged," said Tito. "Fedro is a gypsy mule so naturally he sings in the Caló language." He called upon the gypsies around him. "Reinaldo! Antonio! Roberto!" he shouted. "This gringo says our Caló sounds like the braying of a mule."

The gypsies closed in on the actor. One of them pulled a knife from his sash and felt the blade. "It is just right for slicing the throat of a pig," he said.

Don Alonso tried to back away. "No offense," he said. "It is only that I do not want a braying—a singing mule. I need one that will be content to pull my wagon."

Fedro began braying again. The gypsy men listened to him with rapt faces. "It is perfect Caló," said Roberto. "He sings like my own brother. And this villain says that he brays?"

"No, no," said Don Alonso quickly. "He has a lovely voice. He really should be in opera instead of my poor wandering company."

He tried to break away but the gypsies would not let him.

"You think my mule is not good enough for you because he sings Caló instead of braying like a Spanish mule," said Tito in an insulted voice. "If that is the way you feel about him, I will let you have him for fourteen hundred *pesetas*."

"But I don't want a singing mule," said Don Alonso feebly. "I only want an ordinary mule that I can buy for twelve hundred *pesetas*."

The gypsy with the knife stropped its blade on the actor's cape. "You don't want a mule for fourteen hundred *pesetas* because he is a gypsy mule," he declared darkly.

The actor's eyes followed the knife as if it were a snake. He looked at Fedro and swallowed. "On second thought," he decided, "I have great need for a mule that sings in Caló. I don't know how I got along without one before."

He took some more bills from inside his cape and added them to the others. Tito did not pull his hand away when the bills were offered. He let them fall into his palm and that sealed the bargain.

Don Alonso had a rope thrust into his hand. The gypsies moved on. He was left alone with the mule that sang Caló words.

He looked at Fedro timidly. He didn't know any words

of Caló. He pointed to himself. "Me—Don Alonso. We—go—my—inn—get—wagon. Savvy?"

Fedro was so full of pep that he was ready to go anywhere. He fairly dragged Don Alonso at the end of the rope. He pulled him along the riverbank.

"Whoa! Whoa!" cried the actor in his deepest stage voice. Fedro wouldn't stop so he decided it was because he was not saying it in Caló.

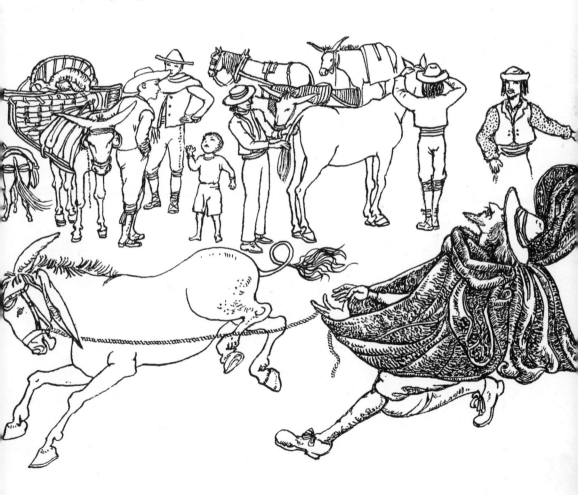

VIII

By shouts and jerks, Don Alonso finally got his mule to the shabby inn on the outskirts of Granada. He guided Fedro into the courtyard, which was filled with old furniture, bulging trunks and pieces of scenery. Everything was jumbled together feet with head.

A pair of mules were rummaging in some straw. A decrepit horse was tied to a wagon wheel. It looked like a skinny, old horse that had escaped from the bullring. The horse whinnied hopefully to Fedro. It was happy to see that at last there was to be some help with the wagon.

Fedro in turn raised his tail, raised his ears and brayed back mournfully. That started a duet by the other mules.

A window was banged open and an untidy woman threw a pail of slops down on the cobbles at Don Alonso's feet. They splashed his cape.

"When are you and your zoo getting out of here?" she demanded.

Other windows opened. A man with a thin mustache leaned over a sagging balcony.

"Hark!" he cried. "Methinks I hear the sound of battle."

A woman with hair that was yellow and red and black at the roots joined him. " 'Tis our brave hero fighting the Moors," she said in a deep, throaty voice.

The untidy woman who owned the inn clanged the bucket against the wall. "If you don't pay your bill and get out of here by noon," she threatened, "I'll call the police."

The horse whinnied again, the other mules started braying and Fedro began singing his saddest Caló words. The untidy woman clapped her hands to her ears. "Give me what you can and get out of here," she cried.

Don Alonso led Fedro to a wagon. He called to a man in a torn blue apron standing by the well.

"Raise the banners," he commanded. "We must away with our brave comrades before yon witch changes her mind. Hitch the new mule behind Rosinante."

He went into the inn, fumbling through the pockets inside his cape.

The man in the torn blue apron buckled Fedro into a harness splendid with frayed tassels and faded rosettes. He put him in front of a bright purple cart, then hitched the horse ahead of him. Perhaps this hurt Fedro's pride. Or

61

perhaps he was sad at leaving Granada. More likely the effect of the snack Tito had given him was wearing off. He didn't feel hot inside any more. He didn't want to fight bulls. He felt tired. His back began to sag. His neck hung. His left ear felt looser than ever. He couldn't even bray because his tail felt so heavy.

When the wagons were packed, Fedro wearily broke into step behind Rosinante. He followed the horse's tail listlessly. Out of the courtyard, down the long dusty road, across the bridge over the River Genil, he followed Rosinante's tail. Behind him creaked the purple wagon with its load of make-believe things. Make-believe trees and doors and walls were packed under the canvas hood.

Even the people in the wagon were make-believe because they were always pretending to be characters in a play. They recited their parts to each and every one they passed. They recited to the flocks of black goats they met, to the brown oxen and the long-tailed sheep.

Mile after mile Fedro followed the horse's tail with his ears full of big words and fine speeches.

They crossed rough mountains with cave houses dug into the barren brown hills. They really were like dog holes or wolf lairs, and the people who lived in them had eyes like wild creatures.

When they reached a village, Don Alonso and his com-

pany would set up the scenery and broken furniture in a
shed or inn courtyard. The man who played the villain took
care of the beasts. It was also his job to go through the
streets and pass out handbills to those who could read
or to describe his goods by word of mouth to those who
couldn't.

"The Traveling Theater is in your midst," he announced.
"A tragedy in three acts will be presented tonight at nine.

63

Never again will you have such an opportunity—and at only five *pesetas* a head."

Fedro and the other mules and the horse would listen to the sounds of the great tragedy as it came from the shed or courtyard that night. They heard a lot of talking and shrieking and scuffling. They heard very little applause from the audience.

Winter was well on the way now so Don Alonso's traveling company stayed in the south of Spain. Fedro pulled the collar to Motril on the blue Mediterranean Sea. They followed a coast that might have been in Africa instead of Spain. It was planted with date and banana groves and fields of sugar cane and carnations.

The air was soft and balmy because the land was sheltered from the cold winds that swept over most of Spain now. Near Almería they came to more rugged scenery with many copper and lead mines along the way. Their road ran below the ruins of old Moorish castles and fortresses.

The Traveling Theater never played in the good-sized towns. Don Alonso sought out the little villages named San This-o or Santa That-a because the people who lived in them were not too particular about their entertainment.

Often they camped in the open with nothing over their heads but the Highway of St. James, as the Spaniards call the Milky Way. And often they were half-starved, the actors as well as their beasts.

"Alas!" sighed Don Alonso. "Poverty stalks our wagons. No one appreciates our great art. These southern peasants have no culture."

One night the traveling players set up their scenery in a large barn. The audience was made up of a few dull peasants who hadn't been to a fiesta for a long time. They sat on rickety benches with their feet buried in the warm straw.

There was a chill from the north in the night air. Fedro thought that he and the other beasts rightfully belonged in the barn. He stood tied to the wagon under the bare stars. He could hear the voices of the actors in their play.

"Please, I beg of thee. Speak to me," came the voice of one of the young men.

"My daughter will never speak again," declared Don Alonso in a harsh voice. "She is dead. And by my own sword."

Then there was the young man's excited voice. "But she is still alive! She moves. She sighs. She is going to speak."

Fedro wanted so much to be in the barn. He raised his ears and he raised his tail. He began his mournful braying.

Gales of laughter came from the barn. Then Don Alonso himself came dashing out in the frayed costume of a Spanish grandee. He carried a wooden sword. He brought it down with all his acting might on Fedro's rump.

"Villain! Rogue!" he shouted. "You have made us the laughingstock of peasants."

Then he returned to the barn and the play went on. But the audience applauded well that night and left in good humor.

It set Don Alonso to thinking. "Perhaps what our show needs is some comedy, my fair Elena," he told the woman with the yellow, red and black hair. "I have a great idea. I happened to remember that the mule sings gypsy songs. We will have him do a song between acts. We will give our audiences something to laugh about if that is what they want—the simpletons."

That is how Fedro became a member of the wandering theater group. It is how he became the star.

At every performance he would sing between the second and third acts of the tragedy. Doña Elena had decided on his costume. She found a torn lace mantilla in one of the bulging trunks. She draped it over his ears and fastened it between them with an artificial rose that had lost half of its petals.

"And now, ladies and gentlemen," Don Alonso would introduce Fedro, "we take great pride in presenting the foremost gypsy singer of Granada, the renowned Mulita." Then Doña Elena would lead Fedro out on the stage with

the mantilla and rose decorating his ears. Don Alonso would pump Fedro's tail and Mulita, the foremost gypsy singer of Granada, would sing "deep song."

How the audience loved it! They rolled off their benches with laughter. They cried, *"Olé!"* and threw their hats and combs up on the stage. What was best, not one of them demanded his money back at the end of the show.

"You were worth every *peseta* I paid that gypsy for you," Don Alonso complimented Fedro. "You really can sing Caló. Our tour will be a triumph."

Fedro was a success on the stage because his singing made everyone laugh. The more they laughed, the sadder grew Fedro's songs. It was the most mournful braying ever heard from a mule.

Fedro was sad because he was a sober, honest mule who had been turned into a clown. He longed for the days when he had been a hard-working beast in San Antonio. In his village every beast, no matter how hard-worked or mistreated by its master, had its dignity, which even the humans respected.

The oxen had their dignity because they were strong at the plow.

The donkeys had their dignity because their burdens were heavy and important.

Even the chickens and turkeys had their dignity because they provided eggs and meat for the hungry workers.

But in this land of make-believe, Fedro had lost his. He had become a low clown.

At last the Traveling Theater reached the proud city of Lorca, noted for its aristocracy and its fine horses.

"They say that even the gypsies here are proud and rich," said Don Alonso. "We will raise the price of our tickets."

He went through the gypsy quarter in person, passing out handbills and announcing that the foremost gypsy singer of Granada would be featured with the wandering players.

He was delighted to see so many gypsies appearing at the innyard that he had rented. They were mostly rich horse dealers and they came carrying their knobbed sticks and whips like royal scepters. Their women wore silken gowns and much gold.

The gypsy audience sat silently through the first two acts of the poor play. They didn't think the actors were very good. They were waiting for the gypsy singer of Granada. What a warm reception they would give her!

"And now, distinguished patrons of the arts," cried Don Alonso, rubbing his soft wet hands together, "I take great pride in presenting Señorita Mulita, the gypsy star. She will sing in your own Caló language."

Onto the stage clopped Fedro with the torn mantilla and

the rose. He stood and looked at his audience sadly. He remembered Granada and the Sacro Monte. He looked for Tito and his children but could not see them.

He raised his tail and raised his ears. He brayed his deepest "deep song."

For a moment there was not a sound from the gypsies.

In the next instant the air seemed filled with bursting firecrackers. The gathering turned into a riot. The insulted

gypsies began breaking up the benches. They knocked the scenery over with their canes. They struck at the fleeing actors with their whips. They raided the box office to get their money back. They gave Fedro such a whipping as no other mule had ever received.

Fedro turned tail and ran out of the innyard. He never looked back once. His ears were turned to the west. He was finished with gypsies and actors.

The long road that led to Granada and Lorca also went back to his native village. He was going home. He was going back to a life of dignity and usefulness.

A mule may not know music or acting or bullfighting, but there is one thing which he knows well. He always knows his way home.

IX

BACK IN SAN ANTONIO, Fedro had not been forgotten. El Bigote and his family and his wife's sister's family had never gotten over the loss of the good strong mule.

The crops hadn't been good that year because there had been no beast to turn the water wheel. The gypsy horse had died in a few days. Many chores had been neglected because there was no mule to help with them. El Bigote had to sell his team of oxen and his goats because there was not enough feed to take them through the winter. Without the oxen he could not lay in firewood. He needed money to feed his families. Without the goats there was not even milk for the children.

Concha still prayed to St. Anthony to find Fedro, and she renewed her vow from time to time. But El Bigote never expected to see the mule again.

"Don't be such a melon," he said to his wife. "Does a

thief return his stolen goods? If the Civil Guards could not find Fedro, neither will prayers and wishes. We are poor now," he declared. "A farmer without beasts is as poor as a dog who has nothing but day and night and the fleas in his coat."

On the Good Night of Christmas Eve, El Bigote and his families went on foot to the church in the square. But there was no feasting when they returned to their home. Small crops, little money, less food.

"Things will get better in the new year," said Concha to cheer them. "The children and I will work in the fields too. We will turn the water wheel."

"And where will you get your strength?" asked El Bigote. "From nibbling the grass on the hillside?"

The new year came at last. It was the year which Concha hoped would make them richer and the year that El Bigote was sure would make them beggars.

The children eagerly waited for Epiphany, the Feast of the Three Kings who went to Bethlehem bearing gifts for the Christ Child.

There are so many Spanish legends that they are in the winds. One of them is that every Epiphany Eve, the Three Kings ride through Spain on their way to Bethlehem. Spanish children fill their shoes with straw for the camels and set them outside the door. In return, the Kings leave gifts for them.

"There is no use in putting your shoes out this year," said Concha to the children. "I have heard that the Three Kings will not come this way. They have found a shorter route to Bethlehem. Spain is really quite out of their way."

The children were disappointed but they did not give up hope. Children have more hope than grownups. El Bigote's children and his wife's sister's children believed that the Kings from the East would pass among their hills.

On the eve of Epiphany they filled their shoes with dried thistles they had picked along the road. They went to the square and joined the other children who were gathering around the fountain. The other children had pockets filled with candy and hands filled with wisps of hay and corn-husks to give the Kings and their camels.

They set out in a band with the grownups laughing and waving encouragement to them, all but El Bigote and Concha.

"The Kings will surely take the road that leads to the mountains," cried one old grandfather. "That is where I met them on Epiphany Eve when I was your age."

"No, no," cried the mayor. "They will take the road to Madrid because there are great festivities awaiting them there."

The children argued among themselves which road to take in order to be sure to meet the Kings. They decided that if they climbed the ox trail past El Bigote's water-

74

wheel and followed the dirt road, they could look into the valley and see the Kings no matter which way they were going.

The sun was setting and the night breezes began to nip their bare legs. El Bigote's children shivered in their ragged clothing. But it was not much colder outside than in their house since there was so little firewood.

They reached the dirt road as the sun sank below the hills. The dusk was deepening into night. How could they see the Three Kings and their camels?

Then the mayor's daughter pointed into the valley. "Look!" she cried. "There they come on their camels."

The children eagerly strained their eyes.

"It is only three hooded wagons," exclaimed the cobbler's son.

"It *is* the Kings," insisted the schoolteacher's little daughter. "Can't you see their golden crowns and rich robes?"

Most of the children began to see the Kings.

"And look at the silver harnesses on their camels," cried the innkeeper's boy.

"See their robes of purple and red and gold!" cried the baker's son.

"And their camels are loaded with saddlebags full of gifts for us," cried the mayor's daughter.

"I don't see anything," insisted the cobbler's son. "And

those hooded wagons have disappeared among the hills. They aren't coming this way."

The children were disappointed. Some of them began eating the candy they had brought for the Kings. Some of them dropped the hay and cornhusks they had brought for the camels.

"They are coming this way," cried the schoolteacher's daughter. "I can hear the hoofbeats of the camels."

All the children listened intently. Clop—clop! The schoolteacher's daughter was right. The Kings were coming up the road toward them. Even the cobbler's son could hear them.

"It's one of the camels," cried the schoolteacher's daughter as a dark beast wearily clopped toward them.

"No, it's a horse," cried the cobbler's son.

"It's a mule," shouted the innkeeper's boy.

"It's Fedro," cried El Bigote's children in one breath.

And it really was Fedro. His coat of hair had grown out again. He had lost his rose in a stream and left his mantilla on the branch of an olive tree. He was the same old Fedro.

El Bigote's children were delighted. They hugged the mule. They welcomed him as if he had been one of the Kings' camels. All the children who had saved their hay and cornhusks gave them to Fedro to eat. And he gulped them down greedily because he was starved.

76

As the children led Fedro back to the village, they chattered about the excitement of the evening. They wanted their parents to feel the same way as they had at sight of the dark, moving objects. The more they talked, the more sure they were that they had seen the Kings on their way to Bethlehem. By the time they reached the village, they believed they had seen Fedro jogging along with the camels.

Concha's eyes grew bigger and bigger as if she were

seeing the gold-crowned Kings on their silver-harnessed camels.

"It is a miracle," she cried. "I prayed to St. Anthony to bring Fedro back and he sent him with the Three Kings."

"Puf!" snorted El Bigote. "He ran away from the gypsies and where was there for him to go but home?"

"He could have gone on to Bethlehem with the Three Kings," lisped his littlest girl.

Concha remembered something. "My vow," she cried. "I must keep the vow I made."

All the village people were curious about Concha's vow.

"Will you burn a hundred candles in the church?" asked the baker's wife.

"I hope you didn't promise money," glowered El Bigote. "If you did, St. Anthony will have to find that for you too."

Concha looked at all the curious faces.

"No, no," she said, "my vow is one that will need the help of everyone in the village." The wide curious eyes narrowed. "I vowed to get everyone to celebrate the blessing of the beasts on St. Anthony's feast day," she announced. "We do not realize how much our beasts mean to us until they are gone. We must do something to show them we appreciate their labor and loyalty."

All the village eyes brightened. They were willing to help with something like this. It would be a holiday for man and beast alike. They had all worked too hard. Man

78

and beast deserved a holiday on the feast of St. Anthony, which was not far away.

The women dug the moss out of the words on the fountain until each letter could be read clearly. The men shined the beasts' bells. They fastened fresh tassels and ribbons to the harnesses. The children bathed and brushed the beasts.

On the morning of the seventeenth of January there was a grand procession of animals toward the square of San Antonio. Fedro led it. Red tassels bounced over his forehead. Bells jingled on his collar. Paper flowers were fastened into his stubby mane and his frayed tail. He walked proudly toward the fountain with his ears held high. He was followed by cows, mules, donkeys and oxen. They were decorated as gaily as Fedro. Horns and ears carried flowers or ribbons. Many long tails were braided with ribbons or golden straw. One horse had the hair on its rump brushed sideways in a checkerboard design.

Droves of pigs and herds of goats and sheep were driven by their masters in the procession. Even old Carlos Moreno led his pig by a string, and his wife drove her three turkeys ahead of her—although one of them ran away and never returned.

The priest headed his own procession of altar boys from the church. He met Fedro at the fountain. He sprinkled beasts and fowls with holy water in the name of St. An-

thony. He blessed their labor and patience.

The rest of the day Fedro was at his ease in the barn while El Bigote's family and his wife's sister's family took it easy in the house and made fine plans for the coming year's work.

"I will take Fedro back into the hills every morning and gather firewood," said El Bigote. "I will go into the firewood business for the winter. By spring we will have enough money to buy another team of oxen and a big flock of goats."

Concha smiled. "I see that you did not keep your vow," she said. "You vowed to give Fedro a beating when he returned."

El Bigote shook his head. "Never again will I mistreat

Fedro or any other beast," he said. "I will always remember the words on the fountain."

So with Fedro home again, prosperity returned to El Bigote's farm. Fedro worked hard and made much money for El Bigote. But nowadays when he raised his head and raised his tail, there was a triumphant tone to his braying. He was proud to be a useful mule.

Then Concha would put her finger to her lips and say to the children, "Hush! Listen to Fedro's beautiful voice! He is singing about his journey with the Three Kings."

About Natalie Savage Carlson

Natalie Savage Carlson was born in Winchester, Virginia, one of a family of seven girls and a boy. Her father was a Union soldier during the War Between the States. When she was eleven, her family moved to California, where Mrs. Carlson completed her education and was a newspaper reporter on the Long Beach *Sun* for two years.

Mrs. Carlson has traveled extensively throughout the United States, Mexico, Canada, and Europe. She lived in Paris for several years with her husband, Captain Daniel Carlson, U.S.N., who was on assignment there.

Among Mrs. Carlson's books are THE TALKING CAT, a Prize Book in the 1952 New York *Herald Tribune* Spring Book Festival; WINGS AGAINST THE WIND, a Prize Book in the 1955 *Herald Tribune* Spring Book Festival; SASHES RED AND BLUE; THE HAPPY ORPHE-LINE; THE FAMILY UNDER THE BRIDGE; A BROTHER FOR THE ORPHELINES; and THE TOMAHAWK FAMILY.

1961